ancy Wilcox Richards • Werner Zimmermann

Farmer Joe
Baby-Sits

Scholastic Canada Ltd.
Toronto, New York, London, Sydney, Auckland

With love, to Jenn and Kris
with special blanket memories.

— N.W.R.

To the mysterious woman
on the plane from Antigua,
Linda Knowles,
and the crazy, zany
and always helpful
Stocktons.

— W.Z.

Scholastic Canada Ltd.
175 Hillmount Road, Markham, Ontario, Canada L6C 1Z7

Scholastic Inc.
555 Broadway, New York, NY 10012, USA

Scholastic Australia Pty Limited
PO Box 579, Gosford, NSW 2250, Australia

Scholastic New Zealand Limited
Private Bag 94407, Greenmount, Auckland, New Zealand

Scholastic Ltd.
Villiers House, Clarendon Avenue, Leamington Spa,
Warwickshire CV32 5PR, UK

Canadian Cataloguing in Publication Data

Richards, Nancy Wilcox, 1958-
    Farmer Joe baby-sits

Issued also in French under title: Pas de dodo sans doudou!

ISBN 0-590-24991-6

I. Zimmermann, Werner. II. Title.

PS8585.I184F3 1997a   jC813'.54   C96-932362-X
PZ7.R52Fa 1997a

6 5 4 3 2   Printed and bound in Canada   9 /9 0 1 2 3 4 /0

Farmer Joe lived with his wife
in an old house
in the middle of a big field.

Most days Farmer Joe
worked hard in the field,
cutting the wheat,
planting the corn
and pulling the weeds.

2

But not today.

Today was a special day.

Farmer Joe was going to baby-sit Jennifer.

Farmer Joe had never done any baby-sitting
before in his whole life!

Jennifer's mother brought a huge bag of toys
and a long list of instructions for Farmer Joe:
    Play lots of games.
    Give Jennifer a snack.
    Make sure she gets outside
    for some fresh air.

And on the very bottom of the list:
    Make sure Jennifer has an afternoon nap.
    She will need her blanket,
    otherwise she WON'T sleep.

Bumpity-bump-bump-bump
went the truck down the dirt road.

Farmer Joe and Jennifer were alone.

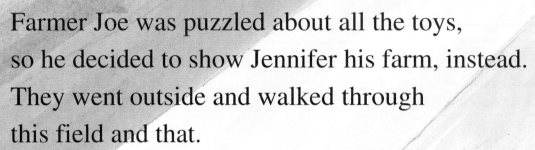

Farmer Joe was puzzled about all the toys,
so he decided to show Jennifer his farm, instead.
They went outside and walked through
this field and that.

They crawled under and over fences.
They climbed up and down ladders.

7

When they got back to the old house
Farmer Joe decided it was time for Jennifer's nap.

But where was her blanket?

He pulled out books, puzzles and dolls,
Tutus, markers and balls . . .
but no blanket.

Jennifer found skates, a hoop and a tea set,
crayons and paints and a helmet . . .
but no blanket.

Oh, no!

"I know," Farmer Joe exclaimed.
"We must have lost your blanket somewhere outside.
It should be easy to find. Let's go!"

Farmer Joe and Jennifer walked through the fields.
They found some corn that needed planting,
and a cow that needed milking,

and a wagon that needed painting . . .
but no blanket.

They found a ladder for climbing,
and a rope for swinging,

and some eggs that needed collecting . . .
but no blanket.

Farmer Joe was worried they would never find it.
Jennifer was *sure* they wouldn't.

But Farmer Joe wouldn't give up.
They walked through this field and that.
They crawled under and over fences.
They climbed up and down ladders.

They searched everywhere . . .
but no blanket.

16

17

"I'm sorry, Jennifer." Farmer Joe sighed.
"I know you can't nap without your blanket,
but there's no place left to look."

Jennifer didn't say anything at all.

Bumpity-bump-bump-bump
came the truck up the dirt road.

Farmer Joe felt a grin coming on.

"Sweet dreams, Jennifer," he whispered.

"Come back any time you like."